DIARY
Wish-a-Day

Star Darlings

Don't miss these other
Star Darlings books

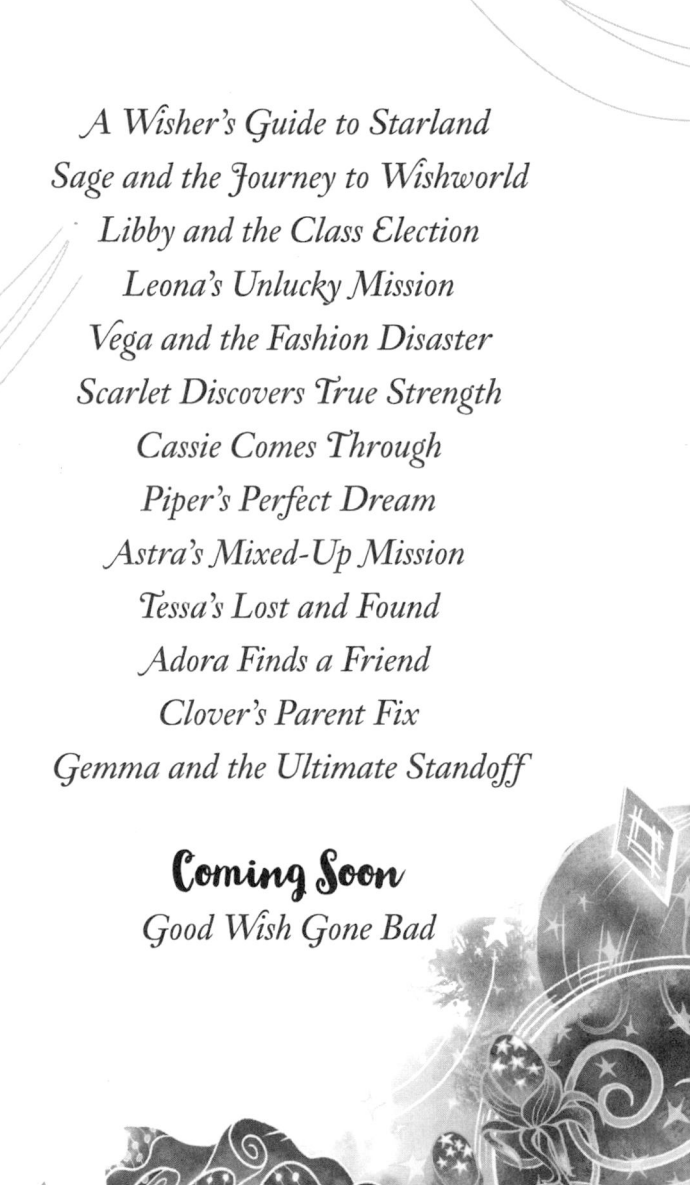

Printed in the United States of America
First Edition, September 2016
1 3 5 7 9 10 8 6 4 2
FAC-008598-16204
Library of Congress Control Number: 2016935513
ISBN 978-1-4847-8217-0
For more Disney Press fun, visit www.disneybooks.com

Star Darlings

Wish-a-Day DIARY

Based on the Star Darlings books
by Shana Muldoon Zappa and Ahmet Zappa

DISNEP PRESS
Los Angeles • New York

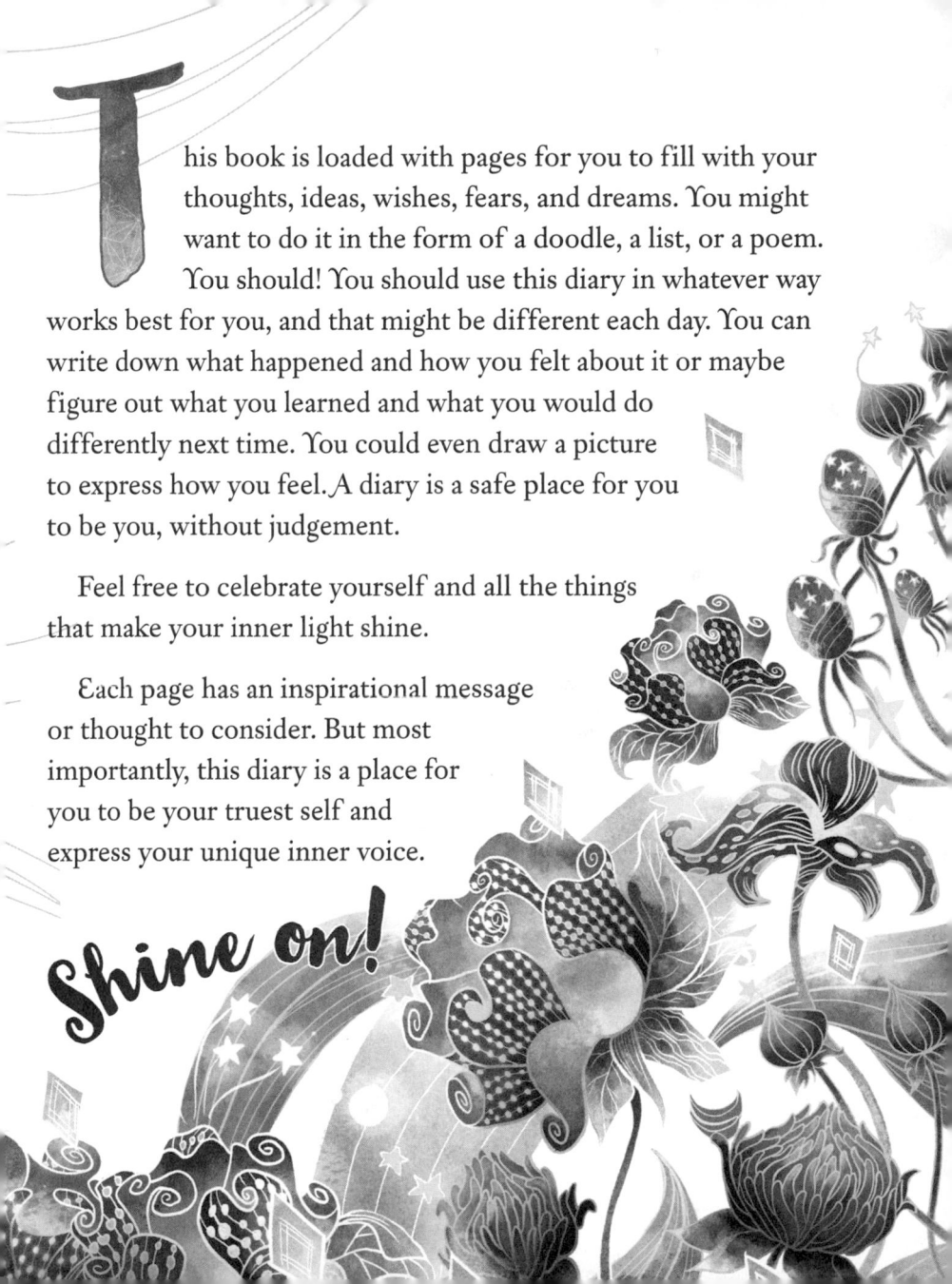

This book is loaded with pages for you to fill with your thoughts, ideas, wishes, fears, and dreams. You might want to do it in the form of a doodle, a list, or a poem. You should! You should use this diary in whatever way works best for you, and that might be different each day. You can write down what happened and how you felt about it or maybe figure out what you learned and what you would do differently next time. You could even draw a picture to express how you feel. A diary is a safe place for you to be you, without judgement.

Feel free to celebrate yourself and all the things that make your inner light shine.

Each page has an inspirational message or thought to consider. But most importantly, this diary is a place for you to be your truest self and express your unique inner voice.

Shine on!

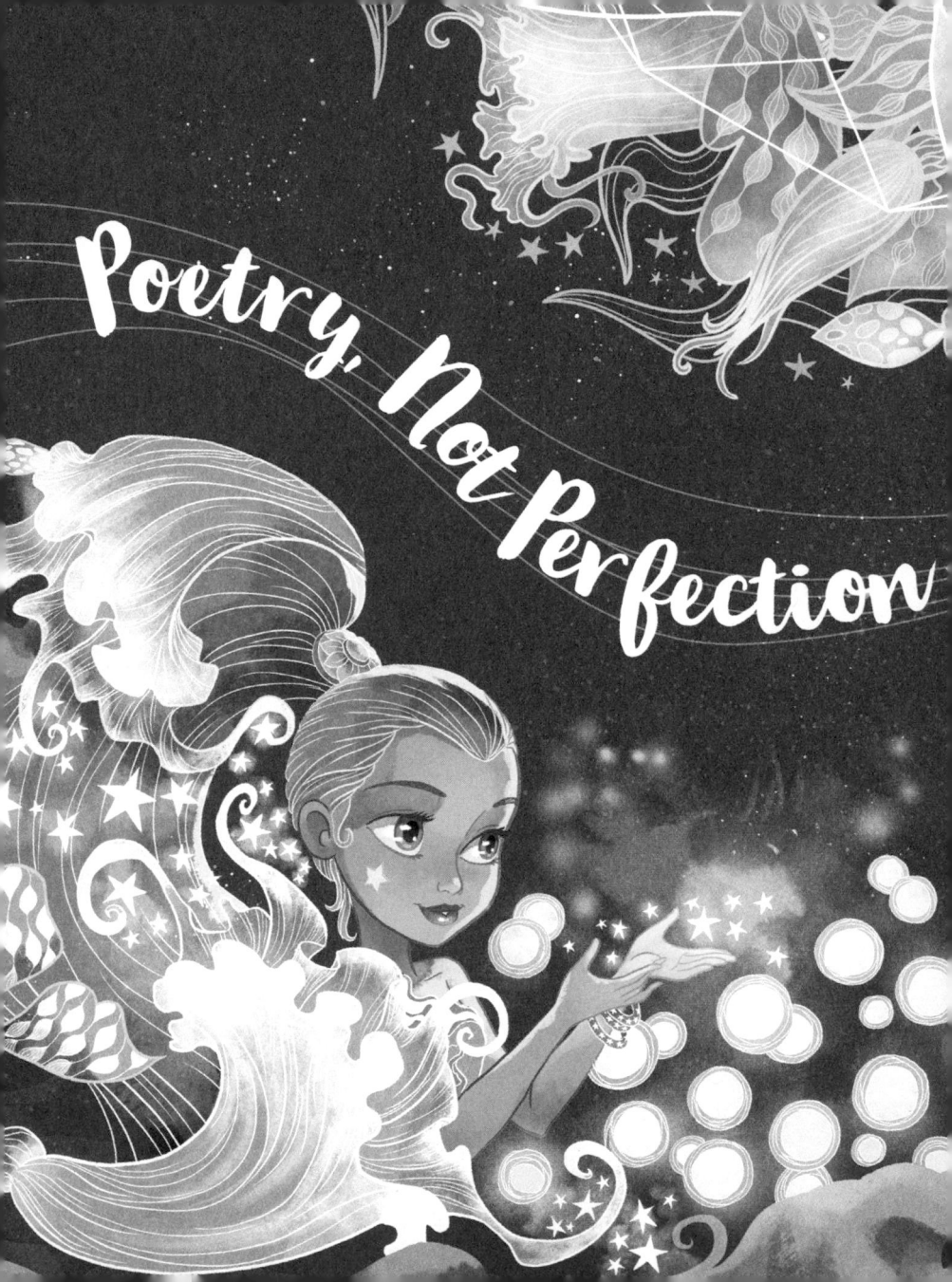

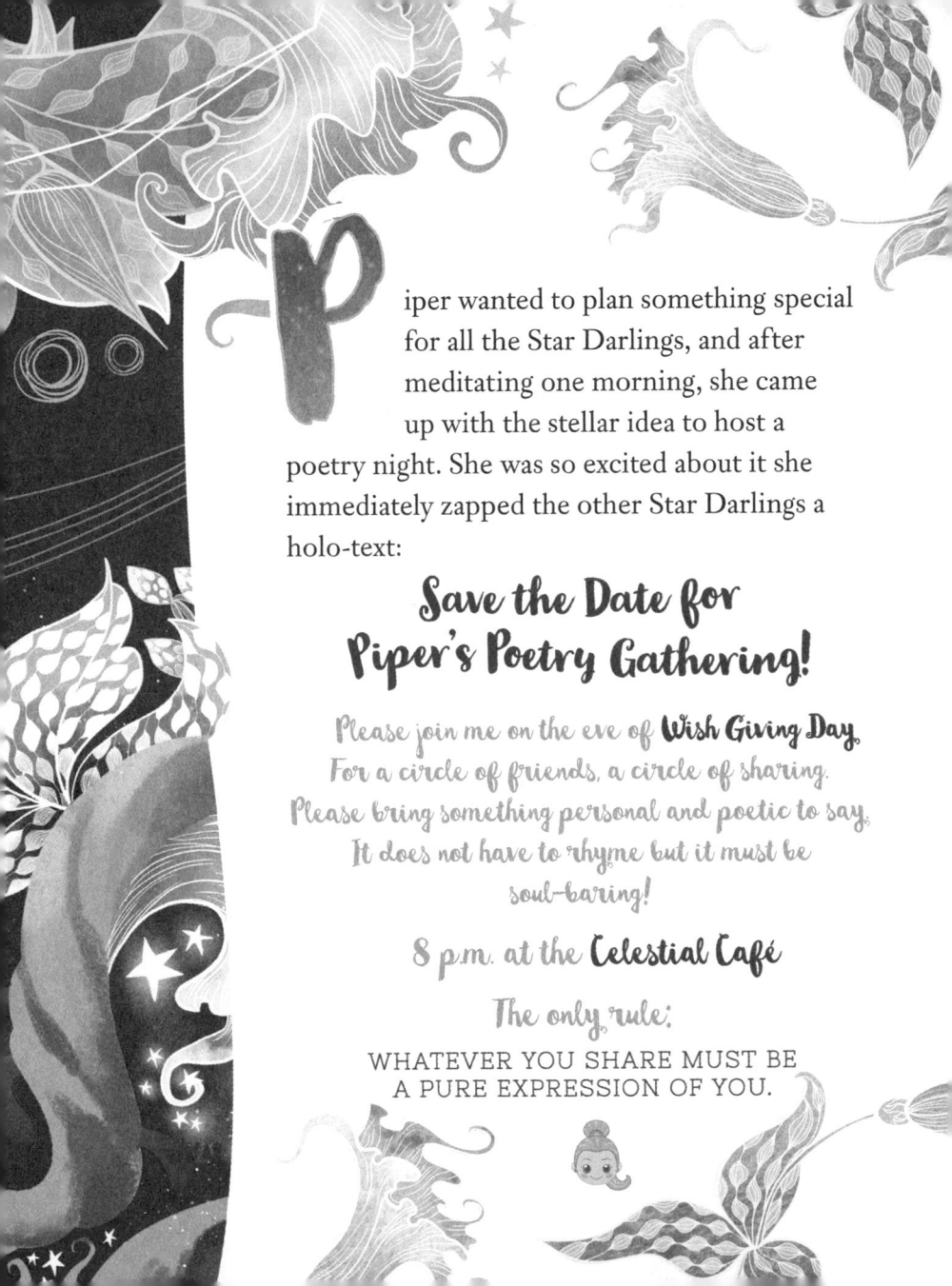

Piper wanted to plan something special for all the Star Darlings, and after meditating one morning, she came up with the stellar idea to host a poetry night. She was so excited about it she immediately zapped the other Star Darlings a holo-text:

Save the Date for Piper's Poetry Gathering!

Please join me on the eve of **Wish Giving Day**,
For a circle of friends, a circle of sharing.
Please bring something personal and poetic to say,
It does not have to rhyme but it must be
soul-baring!

8 p.m. at the **Celestial Café**

The only rule:

WHATEVER YOU SHARE MUST BE
A PURE EXPRESSION OF YOU.

When Piper sent out the holo-text, she was eager to gather her friends in the Celestial Café and use their artistry to create true positive energy!

But as the date loomed closer, there was just one problem: her poem. Piper was obsessing over it, which was unusual for her. She had been working constantly on a whimsical new verse for the occasion, but she found herself rewriting the same three lines of the poem over and over.

She'd write it all the way back to the way it was in the first place, then start changing it all over again. Piper even began to dream about the poem. The lines started to snake around her, binding her so that she couldn't move.

When she had that dream—or any other dream, for that matter—the first thing she always did was reach for her holo-dream journal to write about it. She loved trying to capture

She loved trying to capture the details with words, regardless of whether the dream was good or bad.

the details with words, regardless of whether the dream was good or bad. It helped her make sense of the dreams and what they meant, and when they were scary, it made them less so.

She was hoping the terrible dream wouldn't revisit her the night of the big sleepover that the Star Darlings were having in Libby's room. By that time, Piper had a psychic feeling she was going to be the next Star Darling to go on her Wish Mission, which meant she would have to postpone her poetry night. Honestly, that comforted her. Piper went to sleep hopeful that

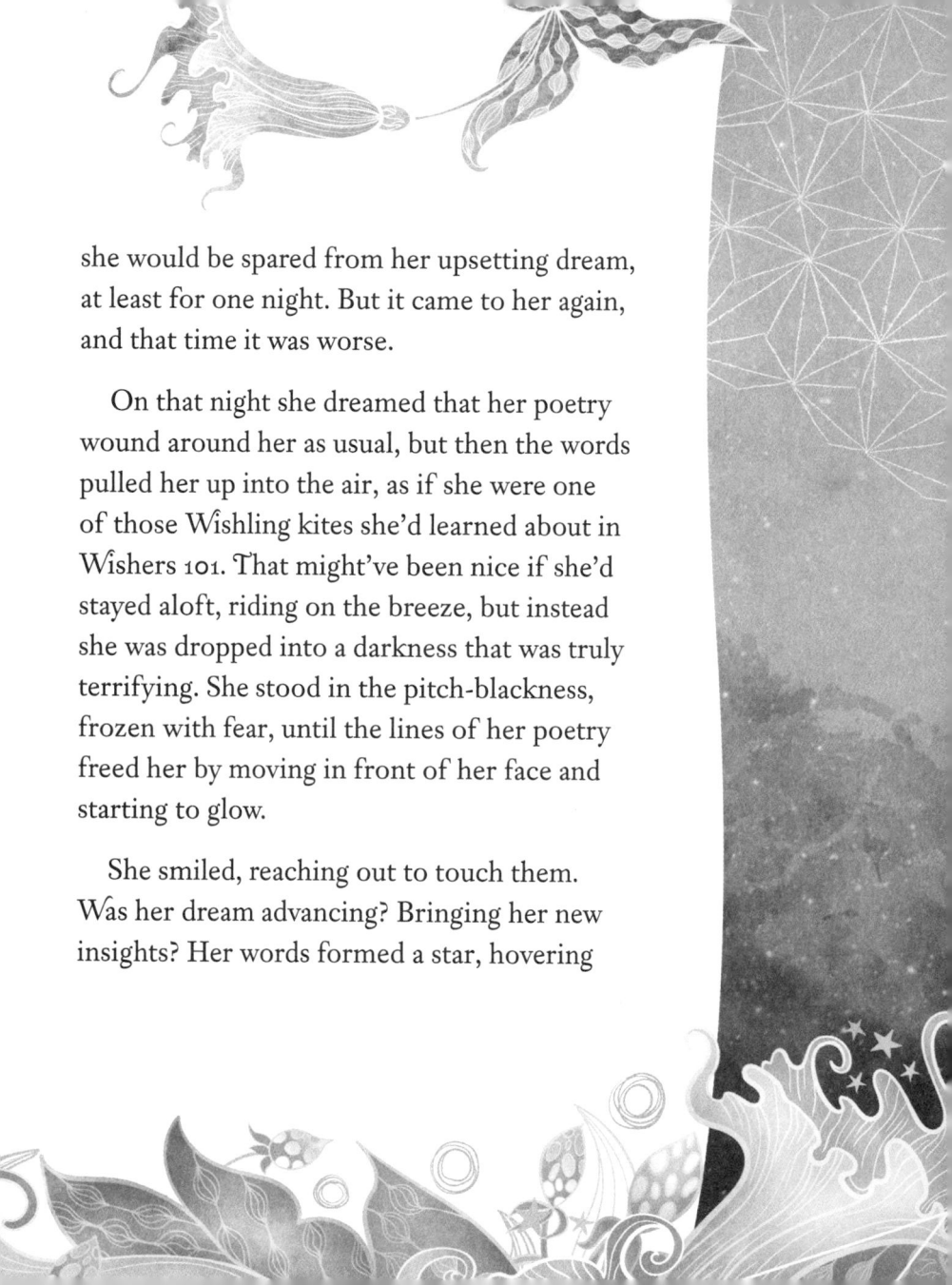

she would be spared from her upsetting dream, at least for one night. But it came to her again, and that time it was worse.

On that night she dreamed that her poetry wound around her as usual, but then the words pulled her up into the air, as if she were one of those Wishling kites she'd learned about in Wishers 101. That might've been nice if she'd stayed aloft, riding on the breeze, but instead she was dropped into a darkness that was truly terrifying. She stood in the pitch-blackness, frozen with fear, until the lines of her poetry freed her by moving in front of her face and starting to glow.

She smiled, reaching out to touch them. Was her dream advancing? Bringing her new insights? Her words formed a star, hovering briefly in front of her before vanishing. Her star! She was to wait there for her star!

She woke with a start.

It happened again the next night, too. Same dream, same poem, same star. Piper wondered if she should she cancel her poetry night. And what about her mission? Would she even make it to Wishworld?

She found out soon enough that her mission to Wishworld was a go. When Lady Stella revealed the Wish Orb had selected her, Piper was elated and relieved. Before she went, she let all the Star Darlings know that her poetry night was on an indefinite hold. Her mission was the perfect cover for what she was really feeling . . . that she didn't know if she'd ever be able to write again, much less share it with anyone in public!

Thankfully, her mission was also a great distraction from her worries. It was total sensory overload—so many different traditions, routines, and customs to discover, not to mention plants, buildings, and people. She especially loved the Wishworld sleepover, which she planned to bring all her new Wishling friends together. It was a magical night, but it made her miss her fellow Star Darlings. She remembered the last sleepover they'd had in Libby's room before she'd come to Wishworld, how she'd encouraged the Star Darlings to hold hands and visualize their Wish Orbs. How she'd sensed the girls' warm smiles. How thrilled they had been to see the rainbow of wish energy they created when all twelve of them held hands. Piper felt a strong wave of sadness overtake her because she hadn't bothered to write about the dream she'd had that night, no matter how scary it had been. Even if it was troubling, it was all part of an important time in her life. And anyway, why did she feel that she only had to write about the dream? What about that celestial sleepover? She realized she'd missed out on writing about the joy she had experienced with the other Star Darlings. That gave Piper another idea; she suggested to her new Wishworld friends that they all make their own journals and put them to good use.

Piper's Wish Mission was a challenge—so much so that Lady Stella sent down some helpful backup by way of Adora—but she did her best to calibrate every effort toward helping out her Wisher. The Wishworld sleepover was a crucial event; it gave her the information she needed to identify the correct wish. So when she finally figured it out, she stole a moment to do some writing. Piper pulled out her brand-new journal. It was very different

Piper and her Wishworld friends had decorated their journals with stickers and drawings and promised to record their wishes and dreams inside.

from a holo-journal. It was made of paper and small enough to fit in her backpack, but it had a comforting weight to it. At the sleepover party, Piper and her Wishworld friends had decorated their journals with stickers and drawings and promised to record their wishes and dreams inside. Piper got out a pen with bright green ink and tried to write down everything that had happened to her on Wishworld, every beautiful thing, every connection, every surprise, every inspiration.

"What was all that writing about?" Adora asked, just before they unfolded their stars to shoot back home. It was then that Piper realized the star she kept seeing in her dream had been a sign after all! It represented the shooting star she rode to Wishworld—her trip was the key to restoring her creative power, and the Wishworld journal had given her the space she needed to express herself freely.

"Just writing. Just for me," Piper replied, and off they went, back to Starland.

Piper's Wishworld journal became her most prized possession when she returned to Starling Academy. She pored over its pages, reliving her wish-granting adventure. She kept writing in it as well, but it confused her, because she had never really kept a journal quite like it. Before she'd left for Wishworld, she'd kept holo-journals: one for poetry and one for recording dreams. She used her dream journal to jot down her subconscious ideas, and her poetry journal, well . . . she didn't always feel like she should fill it up with every last thought she had.

But now she had this Wishling artifact, filled with her scribbles. Part dream diary, part travel diary, some of it was in rhyme, but some of it wasn't even punctuated. She'd done some drawings of things she thought were strange or interesting or memorable, things she just had to explain to the other Starlings but knew she'd never do justice unless she sketched something out. She'd even glued some dried dramboozle leaves onto one of the pages. It was a mess. But it was beautiful!

Piper simply couldn't stop writing in it. Even when she had the option of going back to her holo-journals, she found herself returning to the paper journal and its wrinkled pages, smeared with the strange, smudgy ink that got on her hands when she wrote. It exhilarated and confused her, but she didn't understand why.

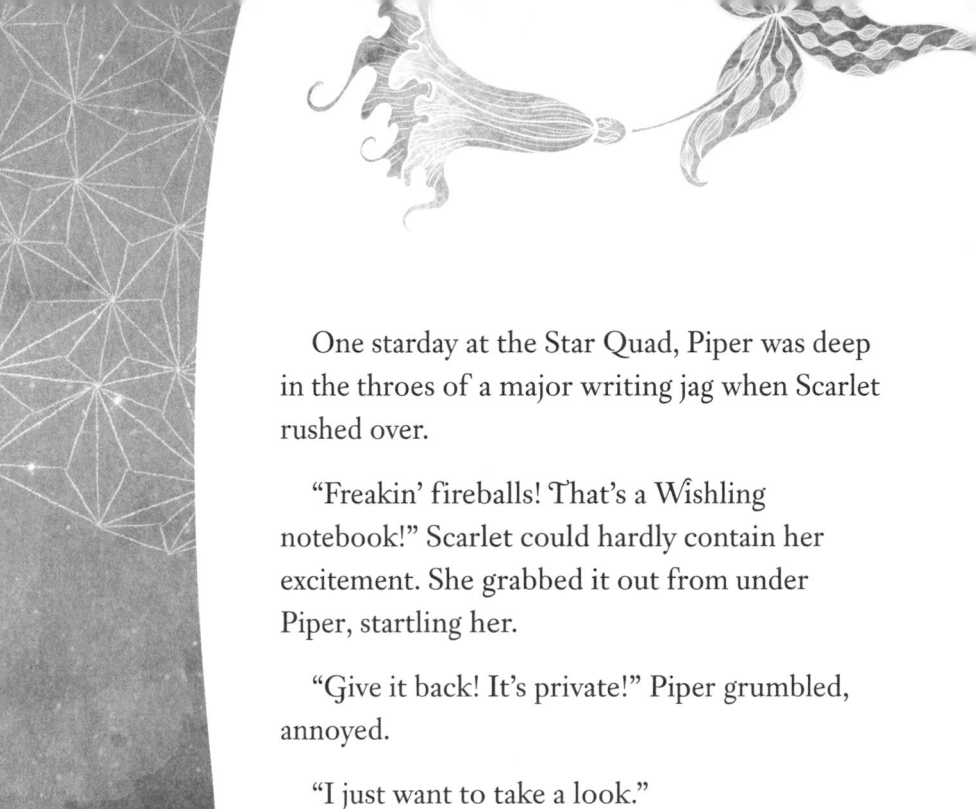

One starday at the Star Quad, Piper was deep in the throes of a major writing jag when Scarlet rushed over.

"Freakin' fireballs! That's a Wishling notebook!" Scarlet could hardly contain her excitement. She grabbed it out from under Piper, startling her.

"Give it back! It's private!" Piper grumbled, annoyed.

"I just want to take a look."

Piper relaxed . . . a little. "Okay, just don't read anything."

"Do you have more?" Scarlet asked her.

"Sorry, no. That's the only one."

"That's too bad. It's super celestial. All these drawings inside! And wow, you're writing all over the place, aren't you? In the margins, words "around words—"

Piper snatched it back out of Scarlet's hands. "Okay, that's enough."

"Why the Wishling notebook?" Scarlet asked. "You could write in a holo-book and keep this in perfect condition if you wanted."

"I don't know. I started it on Wishworld and I can't seem to stop."

"So you probably have tons of stuff to share at poetry night. *You are* rescheduling it, aren't you?"

Piper looked unsure. "I . . . I don't know."

"You've got to," Scarlet insisted. "And you've got to share this notebook, too. Show some of your artwork and read from it. It's an amazing souvenir of your Wishworld adventure! And it's traveled all this way back with you."

"I can't."

"Why not?"

"It's not meant to be shared. And I don't know . . . I'm thinking of canceling poetry night. . . . Anyway, I have to go." Piper stood and stormed off, leaving behind a confused Scarlet.

Back in her dorm, Piper sat in front of her Wishworld journal. She wanted to pick up where she'd left off, but after all that talk from Scarlet, she felt anxious and bound up, just like in her dream. She tried to let the words flow from the pen, like she'd been able to do with such ease ever since she got back from Wishworld, but nothing came. She turned to her poetry holo-journal, with its unfinished poem. She wished she could just finish it.

First she tried meditating. She sat in the center of the room, visualizing words and images spilling from her fingertips like water, like steam, like a rainbow of positive energy. As hard as she tried, however, she couldn't maintain the vision; the water froze, the steam evaporated, the rainbow disappeared.

"Starf!" she shouted just as Vega walked in.

"Sorry to bother you, Piper."

"No, I'm sorry. I'm just . . . frustrated."

"With what?"

"I felt like I was finally getting back to writing again. And even getting better at it! And

She sat in the center of the room, visualizing words and images spilling from her fingertips like water . . .

then Scarlet started telling me I had to share it at my poetry night—"

"What's wrong with that?"

"I don't know! I just know the minute she started talking about me having to share it with anybody I couldn't do it anymore! I mean, before I couldn't finish the poem because I wanted it to be perfect and it wasn't. And now I can't write in my new journal because I started out thinking it didn't have to be anything special, but if I have to share it, it has to be perfect!"

"Blazes, Piper, you're starting to sound like me, wanting everything to be perfect," Vega said, walking into her part of the room. "I think you should have poetry night and I think you should share whatever you want. I've been working on a series of lightkus and every syllable needs to be perfect on those. But the only reason I started working on them was because of your poetry night!"

Piper stood and walked out, frustrated.

Serenity Gardens seemed the next best place for her to center herself and figure out how to get back to doing the thing she loved to do. She felt certain that she was a writer, but how could she write if she didn't think it was good enough? Once again, she closed her eyes and tried to imagine herself channeling poetry and positive energy. But instead her mind took her back to her Wishworld journey, that thrilling star ride, the struggle to succeed, and Adora's appearance. *Adora!*

She opened her eyes and there was Adora. It was almost as if she had conjured her, merely by recalling that fond memory of their Wishworld partnership.

"There you are!" Adora said, pleased. She was holding a holo-book, as if she had something urgent to share. "I wanted to show you this startastic new outfit I'm designing for your poetry night—"

"But I'm postponing—"

"A new outfit for *you*. I know you want to postpone again. I'm going to make you look confident to help you *feel* confident. All you need is a little boost!"

"No, that's not all I need! What I need is for my poetry to be for me again. That's the whole problem. Planning poetry night made me too critical of my writing because I was doing it for other people. Remember when we were about to take off from Wishworld together? What I said was just for me. That's what I need writing to be."

"It still can be, Piper."

"How do you mean?"

"This outfit I'm making. You might wear it, but it's my outfit. My expression. It's mine and I love it! And I have dozens of things I'm working on that are just as much mine that I'm not going to show you. And that's okay."

"Of course, but—"

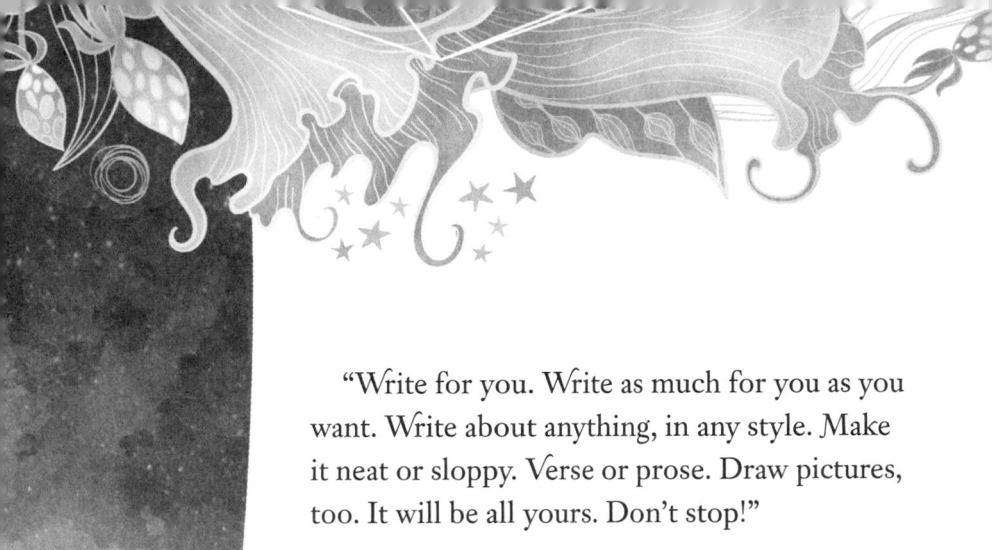

"Write for you. Write as much for you as you want. Write about anything, in any style. Make it neat or sloppy. Verse or prose. Draw pictures, too. It will be all yours. Don't stop!"

"Yeah, but then what?"

"Pick out a few things you think we'll like, and share them with us. That's all you have to do."

"But it has to be good!"

"It has to be *you*. That's all. Now get back to your writing."

"I'll try," Piper said with a sigh.

"Good," Adora replied, then turned to her holo-book. "Now check out this outfit. I think you're really going to like it!"

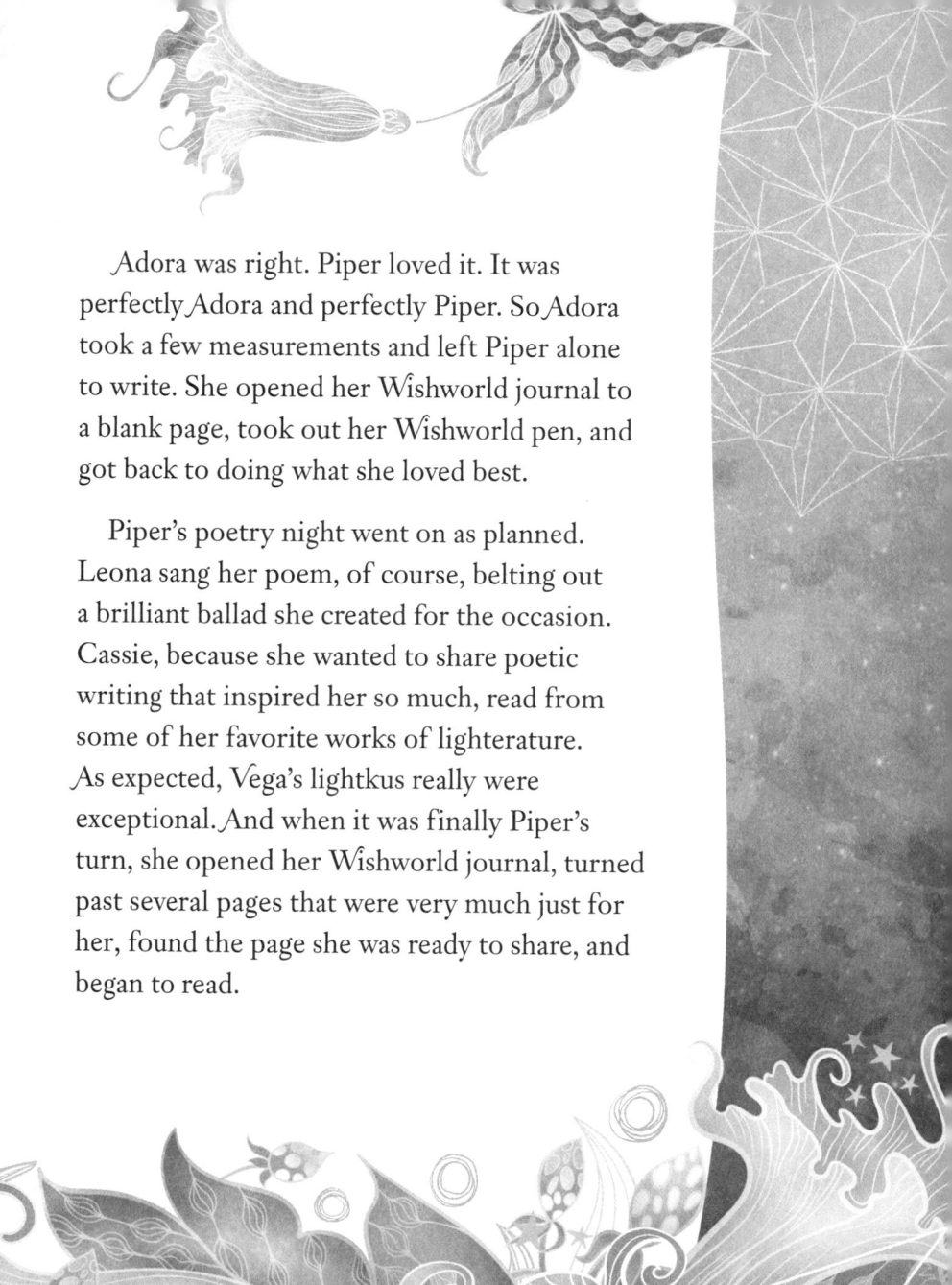

Adora was right. Piper loved it. It was perfectly Adora and perfectly Piper. So Adora took a few measurements and left Piper alone to write. She opened her Wishworld journal to a blank page, took out her Wishworld pen, and got back to doing what she loved best.

Piper's poetry night went on as planned. Leona sang her poem, of course, belting out a brilliant ballad she created for the occasion. Cassie, because she wanted to share poetic writing that inspired her so much, read from some of her favorite works of lighterature. As expected, Vega's lightkus really were exceptional. And when it was finally Piper's turn, she opened her Wishworld journal, turned past several pages that were very much just for her, found the page she was ready to share, and began to read.

The best part about wishes is
there are no impossibilities

DATE

Date

I am . . .

"I AM," are two of the most powerful words,
because what you put after them creates your reality.

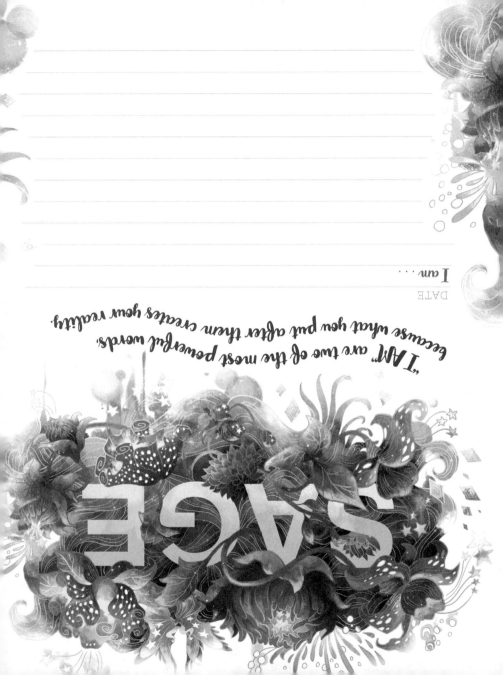

SAGE

Date

never let go!

AND

HOLD ON TO THE THINGS THAT MAKE YOU HAPPY,

DATE

Even though people might try to break you, or shake you,
never forget what MAKES YOU.

LEONA

Date

DON'T BE AFRAID TO *live out loud!*

Date

At the heart of success is passion.

_____
_____
_____
_____
_____
_____
_____
_____
_____
_____
_____
_____

DATE

The only way an idea will work
is if you do.

DATE

Be yourself. Be bold. Be unique.

Date _____

TOUGH TIMES NEVER LAST,
but tough people do!

DATE

You can admire someone's greatness without questioning your own.

ASTRA

Date

FAILURE IS AN OPPORTUNITY TO BEGIN AGAIN.

What's your next beginning?

Date

Collect moments, not things.

_____

_____

_____

_____

_____

_____

_____

_____

_____

_____

_____

DATE

Loving someone takes courage.
Start with yourself and you will never lose.

Date

Connect with someone through laughter today.

DATE

Life doesn't have to be about finding yourself.
It can be about creating yourself.

It's okay to make mistakes.
Just remember your mistakes don't make you.

DATE

Date

You can choose to have an awesome day. Try it!

Date

You have the power
to either change things
or let them go.

Rule your world,
not the other way around!

Find something special in everyone.

DATE

Date

Don't let
your fears keep you from
experiencing life.

Look at the things you create as an extension of yourself,
and you will always strive for greatness.

VEGA

It's better to be real than to be perfect.

You can find something good in every day.
Try it!

PIPER

Date

DON'T CONFINE YOURSELF BY BUILDING WALLS

around you.

DATE

Be bold about your wishes.
Share them with your friends and your family!

Date

So make it count.

YOU'LL NEVER GET A
DO-OVER ON TODAY,

Date

Your world is for you to shape.
And color. And create. What kind of
artist will you be?

_____
_____
_____
_____
_____
_____
_____
_____
_____
_____
_____
_____
_____
_____
_____
_____

DATE

Remember that the people who belong in your life will be there to stay.

Don't always follow a pattern.
Make your own design.

You can be fashion-forward,
but never forget your past.

ADORA

Deep down, you always
knew the truth.

DATE

Date

spend time with
BE THE PERSON WHO YOU WOULD LOVE TO

Date

NOTHING IS BEYOND
your capabilities.

Date

Winning isn't everything . . .
but it does feel good!

Date

help today

SAVING KINDNESS FOR TOMORROW DOESN'T

DATE

If you are comfortable in your own skin,
that self-confidence will shine through.

LIBBY

Date

ALWAYS FIND TIME FOR THE THINGS THAT MAKE YOU
HAPPY TO BE ALIVE. WHAT ARE YOUR TOP

happy-to-be-alive things?

Comparing yourself to someone else can steal your joy. Be grateful that you are unique.

Remember any struggle you experience
is an important part of your story.

DATE

Date

Everything happens for a reason. What can you learn from it?

While on the road to success, be sure to stop and enjoy life's comforts along the way.

TESSA

We all have superpowers.

Date

EVERY ONCE IN A WHILE IT'S OKAY TO BREAK A RULE.
LET YOUR CONSCIENCE BE YOUR GUIDE.

Practice patience.
Some things are well worth the wait.

DATE

Date

Do you have a skill or talent
that you've perfected through hard work
and dedication?

Date

hopes and dreams

TO BE A FAILURE ISN'T TO FAIL
BUT TO GIVE UP ENTIRELY.
NEVER GIVE UP ON
YOURSELF OR YOUR

Do you have psychic powers?
Have you shared them with others?

Date

UNDERSTAND YOURSELF FIRST AND THEN YOU CAN

understand others.

Date

Quit overthinking your first instinct is usually the right one.

Believing that you can
is half the battle.

DATE

Remember, you are only responsible for changing yourself—nobody else.

LEONA

Date

How determined are you?

AN AIMLESS FOLLOWER IS DETERMINATION

THE DIFFERENCE BETWEEN A STRONG LEADER AND

DATE

The best thing you can call yourself
is a friend.

Date _____

IF YOU'VE NEVER FAILED, YOU'VE PROBABLY
NEVER TRIED. NAME SOMETHING THAT
YOU'VE TRIED AND THEN FAILED.

What did you learn about yourself in the process?

NEVER CHANGE WHO YOU ARE FOR
OTHER PEOPLE. BE YOUR TRUE SELF AND
THE RIGHT PEOPLE WILL LOVE

the real you.

Date

Date

Dreams don't
have to die. You can always
turn them into plans.

DATE

What do you love about
competition?

Once you turn your "can'ts" into "cans,"
you'll see what you're capable of.

Date _____

_____

_____

_____

_____

_____

_____

_____

_____

_____

_____

_____

THE TINIEST BIT OF KINDNESS CAN
CHANGE SOMEONE'S DAY. HOW MANY ACTS
OF KINDNESS CAN YOU ACCOMPLISH *this week?*

DATE

One thing you can give and
yet always keep is your word.

DATE

You will never know what you can achieve
until you take the leap and try.

Date

Sometimes bringing a bit of faith to a sad situation is exactly what's needed.

Date

LAUGH OFTEN—and loudly.

Do you consider yourself a "born performer"? Why?

DATE _____

_____
_____
_____
_____
_____
_____
_____
_____
_____
_____

CLOVER

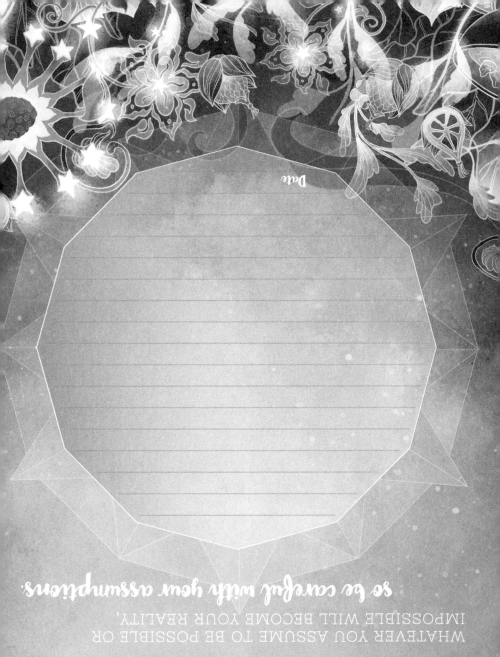

Date

WHATEVER YOU ASSUME TO BE POSSIBLE OR
IMPOSSIBLE WILL BECOME YOUR REALITY,
so be careful with your assumptions.

_____

_____

_____

_____

_____

_____

_____

_____

_____

DATE

Inspiration isn't always flowing. We all need time to fill up the well once in a while.

Date

If your outlook
is positive, your future will
shine bright.

Date _____

_____

_____

_____

_____

_____

_____

_____

_____

_____

_____

_____

_____

that matters most.

IT'S WHAT YOU LEARN
ABOUT YOURSELF DURING
THE TOUGH TIMES

What inspires you to work harder than anyone else?

DATE

If your to-do list is getting you down,
it's time for a dance break.

Date

DO YOU EMBRACE YOUR UNIQUENESS,
OR DO YOU WISH YOU WERE
just like anyone else?

Date

If you look through
the rain long enough, you will see
a rainbow.

DATE

How do **YOU** show the world
that you're confident?

Date

Let yours be known.

EVERYONE HAS NATURAL TALENTS.

DATE

If it's important enough to you,
you'll find a way to make it work.

There's nothing wrong with craving the spotlight.
Think of a time when all eyes were on you and
you loved every minute of it.

LEONA

DATE

Wish one size too big.

Date

List five times
when your problem-solving skills came in
handy recently.

NOT EVERYBODY IS TOUCHY-FEELY, BUT THAT
DOESN'T MEAN YOU'RE COLD AND PRICKLY.
REMEMBER THAT AND IT MAY EASE YOUR WORRIES
about making friends.

Date

What's something that
you rebelled against recently?

SOMETIMES THE MOST ANNOYING TASK BECOMES
EASIER WHEN YOU DO IT WITH SOMEONE ELSE.

Who is your go-to teammate?

Date _____

Be clear on what you want. That's the first step you need to take to get it.

ASTRA

Date

You can help people by simply giving them an opportunity to help themselves.

YOUR ATTITUDE IS LIKE A BOOMERANG:
WHATEVER YOU PROJECT OUT INTO THE WORLD
comes right back to you.

_____

_____

_____

_____

_____

_____

_____

_____

_____

_____

_____

Date _____

Date

WHAT'S YOUR FAVORITE WAY TO MAKE
those around you laugh?

It's okay to talk about
nothing sometimes.

DATE

A great friend is loyal and kind and true.
Are you a great friend?

DATE
_____
_____
_____
_____
_____
_____
_____
_____
_____
_____

CLOVER

DATE

If you have a day when you feel small
and insignificant, remember that you are
someone's everything

Date

Discover what interests you,
then go and do it. Now watch yourself grow
in ways you never imagined.

No problem is insurmountable.

If you're afraid to say it out loud, try writing it down.
Expressing yourself in any form is important.

THE MOST EFFECTIVE WAY TO
GET SOMETHING DONE IS TO
SET YOUR SIGHTS ON IT
and do it.

_____
_____
_____
_____
_____
_____
_____
_____
_____
_____
_____

Date _____

_____
_____
_____
_____
_____
_____
_____
_____
_____
_____
_____

DATE

There are many roads to success, so if one doesn't get you there, another will.

VEGA

Date

strive for progress.

WHILE PERFECTION MAY BE YOUR GOAL,
YOU CAN ALWAYS

DATE _____

Always be ready
for the next adventure.

Do you have a knack for writing poetry?
If not, give it a try. It's a great way to express your feelings.

PIPER

DATE

Don't be afraid to say how you feel.
Those who care about you are ready to listen.

Date

LOVE + UNDERSTANDING = *true friendship.*

Believing in yourself leads to unbelievable things.
What unbelievable things can you dream up?

Date

AMAZING!

THE BEST REVENGE
FOR A BAD YESTERDAY
IS TO MAKE TODAY

Date

YOU WILL FIND HAPPINESS WHEN YOU ARE THE
FORCE THAT MAKES *something happen.*

ADORA

Do you make decisions by analyzing the facts, or do you go with your emotions?

Date

IT'S WHEN YOU FACE YOUR FEARS THAT YOU

gain confidence.

It's your life,
so make your own music.

DATE

You do you!

Date

Know your strengths
and use them to get you
where you want to go.

DATE

You'll see the same people on your rise to the top as you will if you fall. Be nice to them always.

LIBY

DATE

Success can't be measured
in things.

Date

It's contagious.

NEVER UNDERESTIMATE THE POWER OF ENTHUSIASM

DATE _____

If you give trust, you will earn respect.

Date

If someone gives you a
reason to cry, remember that you have
many reasons to smile.

Date

A LESSON LEARNED HELPS
YOU GROW IN INFINITE WAYS.
WHAT LESSONS HAVE YOU
LEARNED LATELY?

TESSA

It's your life, and no one can tell you your truth but you.

DATE

Date

Invite a Friend!

A GRAND ADVENTURE.
WHAT ARE YOU CURIOUS ABOUT? TURN IT INTO
CURIOSITY IS ANOTHER WORD FOR ADVENTURE.

The only opinion of you that matters is your own.
Make a list of what you love about yourself.
Look at it often.

Date _____

YOUR VOICE LETS
THE WORLD KNOW
you exist.

Date

Remember that pressure makes diamonds. Never give up!

_____

_____

_____

_____

_____

_____

_____

_____

_____

_____

DATE

Share what makes you sparkle
with others.

Date

starting something new.

IF YOU'RE TOO AFRAID TO START, YOU'RE ALREADY
FINISHED. DON'T LET FEAR STOP YOU FROM

Dream. Wish. Believe.

DATE

IT'S OKAY TO BE EXCITED.
IN FACT, IT'S AWESOME.
Enjoy it!

Date

_____

_____

_____

_____

_____

_____

_____

_____

_____

_____

_____

_____

_____

_____

_____

_____

_____

_____

_____

_____

_____

_____

A positive attitude will only
make things better.

_____
_____
_____
_____
_____
_____
_____
_____
_____
_____
_____
_____
_____
_____
_____
_____
_____
_____
_____
_____

DATE

*The only way
to start something
is to simply begin.*

Date

Be an original, not an echo.

Don't just think of great ideas. Put them to work.
You may just amaze yourself.

ADORA

Do not be discouraged by mistakes.
They are part of the experience.

Date

Here's a secret:
you are braver and smarter
than you think.

IT'S NOT NECESSARY TO BOAST ABOUT
YOUR ACCOMPLISHMENTS—

they speak for themselves.

_____

_____

_____

_____

_____

_____

_____

_____

_____

_____

_____

Date _____

THE DIFFERENCE BETWEEN
WINNING AND LOSING IS COMMITMENT.
COMMIT TO THE JOURNEY AND SEE WHERE IT

takes you.

Date _____

DATE

You can inspire others with your passion,
so share it with the world.

LIBBY

*Think of every new person or experience
as a door to a different world.*

DATE

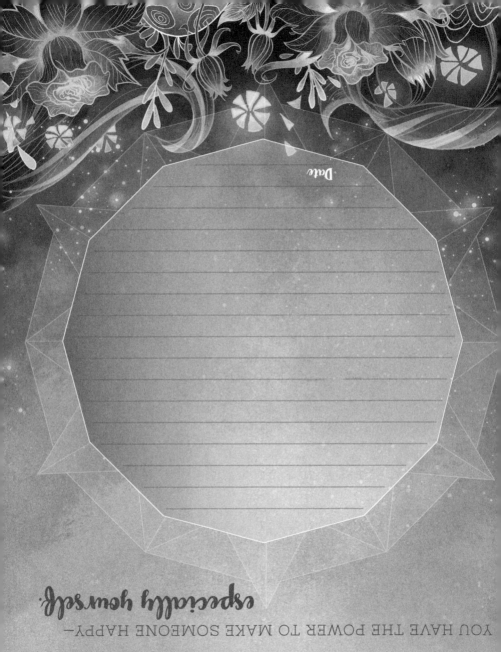

Date

YOU HAVE THE POWER TO MAKE SOMEONE HAPPY—
especially yourself.

DATE

"There's no need to put life on "repeat."
Make every day a special day."

DO YOU EVER FIND YOURSELF TALKING TO CREATURES THAT CAN'T TALK BACK, JUST TO MAKE SURE

you've been heard?

Date

Date

Even heroes get scared sometimes.
The difference between a hero and a coward is a
coward quits and a hero keeps going.

DATE

Happiness can't be found in material things.
It lives in your heart.

DATE

If you work hard, you should be able to play
just as hard. What's your favorite way to play?

Don't waste time wallowing in regret.
Life is too short for that.

DATE

TESSA

DATE

The sweetest way to make a great friend
is to be a great friend.

Date _____

IT'S OKAY TO PUT ALL OF YOUR EGGS IN ONE BASKET.
IF THE BASKET BREAKS, SIMPLY
get a new one.

MAKE A LIST OF THE THINGS
YOU WANT TO ACCOMPLISH
THIS MONTH, THEN FEEL THE
JOY EACH TIME YOU GET TO
CROSS SOMETHING
off your list.

_____

_____

_____

_____

_____

_____

_____

_____

_____

Date _____

Date

You won't fall
behind if you're always
looking ahead.

_____ Date

_____

_____

_____

_____

_____

_____

_____

_____

_____

_____

_____

_____

_____

_____

_____

open your eyes.

YOU CAN SEE AMAZING THINGS WHEN YOU

It's not weak to admit you have weaknesses;
it's honest. Take comfort in knowing
that everyone has them.

If you think highly of yourself,
the world will, too.

DATE

Date

Act on your ideas.
If you don't, nobody will.

Date

who you are.

YOU DO NOT NEED ANYONE'S APPROVAL TO BE

No matter how far you've come,
never forget where you started from.

LEONA

Date _____

DO YOU OBSESS ABOUT **the details?**

Remember, there are no stupid questions, so just ask.

DATE

If you're feeling like everyone's against you,
make sure you're not standing in your own way.

SCARLET

There are two sides to every argument,
so pick your battles.

Date

Every winner knows exactly
what losing feels like. Don't be afraid to lose
on your way to winning.

COOPERATION IS WHEN YOU FEEL
COMFORTABLE SHARING IDEAS
AND KEEPING YOURSELF

open to new ones.

Date

Choose your friends wisely.
You will be judged by the company you keep.

DATE

LIBBY

Date

GOOD FRIENDS HELP EACH OTHER *to be great.*

Date

It's nice to be
important, but it's more
important to be nice.

Who's the chatty one in your group of friends?

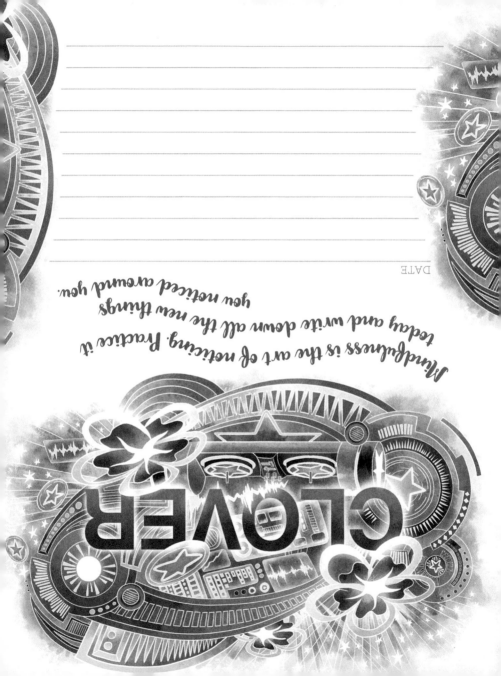

Mindfulness is the art of noticing. Practice it today and write down all the new things you noticed around you.

DATE _____

CLOVER

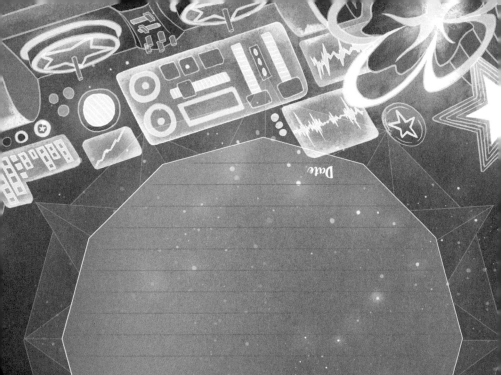

Date

Celebrate differences.

EVERYONE IS DIFFERENT.
THAT'S WHAT MAKES THE WORLD GO ROUND.

Date _____

_____

_____

_____

_____

_____

_____

_____

_____

_____

_____

_____

_____

SOMETIMES YOU HAVE TO SAY,

"**Why not!**"

Date

How have you
shown loyalty to your family
and friends?

People decide how to treat you
based on what treatment you accept.

DATE

Every girl needs adventures to guide her to where she truly belongs. What's your next one?

CASSIE

Set the bar high and
know it's not a ceiling.

Date

They won't go anywhere.

IF YOU'RE OVERWHELMED, IT'S OKAY TO LET
YOUR GOALS HAVE A DAY OFF.

Date

Let your dreams show you the way.

Strength comes when you are able
to love yourself and be yourself.

DATE

You can't please everyone all of the time,
so don't waste your time trying.

Date

IF YOU KEEP
YOUR HEAD UP AND
YOUR EYES AND EARS OPEN,
YOU'LL GET THERE.

DATE

If you get on the dance floor,
chances are someone else will, too.

LEONA

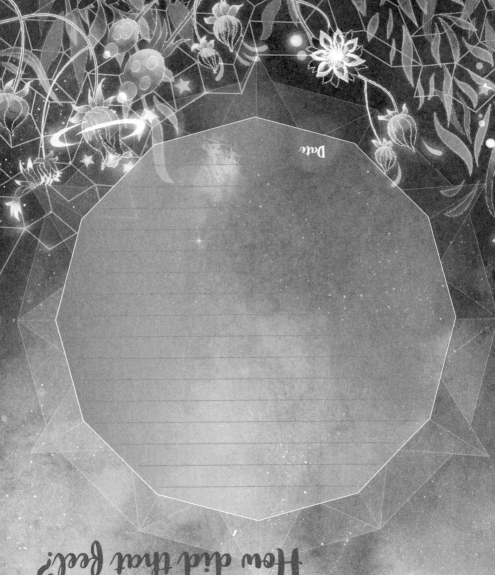

Date

How did that feel?

EVER THROWN YOUR PLAN OUT THE WINDOW AND
GONE WITH THE FLOW?

THE VERY ACT OF BELIEVING IN YOURSELF
GIVES YOU STRENGTH. WHEN WAS THE LAST TIME
YOU BELIEVED YOU COULD DO SOMETHING?

_____

_____

_____

_____

_____

_____

_____

_____

_____

_____

_____

_____

Date _____

Date

Listen well instead of reading fast.

DATE

All accomplishments have one thing in common: they all started with the courage to try.

DATE

Don't feel bad about your past.
You don't live there anymore.

SCARLET

Have the courage to make
something great happen.

Date

ARE YOU TYPICALLY LASER-FOCUSED ON WINNING,
OR ARE YOU CONTENT
just having fun?

_____

Never be too busy to help
those around you.

Date

What's one thing
you can do today that your future self
will thank you for?

BE WILLING TO ADMIT YOUR FLAWS.
THERE'S NO SHAME IN THAT. AND IT MIGHT
JUST MAKE OTHERS COMFORTABLE ENOUGH
to admit theirs.

Date

Do you ever feel lonely even when
you're surrounded by people?
Why do you think that is?

NEVER WORRY ABOUT BEING DIFFERENT
FROM THE PACK.
That's what makes you
YOU.

_____

_____

_____

_____

_____

_____

_____

_____

_____

_____

Date _____

DATE

A true friend will dance with you in the
sunshine and walk with you in the darkness

Date

A real friend accepts you just the way you are.

Date

IF CHANGING THE WORLD SEEMS
TOO DAUNTING, REMEMBER THAT
YOU CAN ALWAYS CHANGE

the world in you.

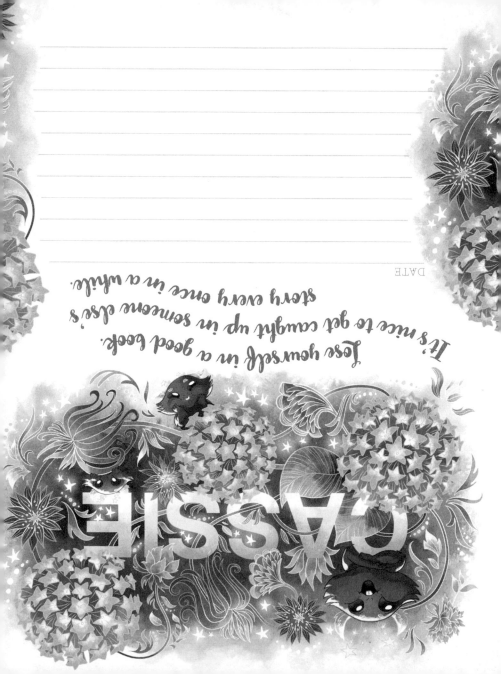

Lose yourself in a good book.
It's nice to get caught up in someone else's
story every once in a while.

CASSIE

If you speak clearly and from the heart,
you cannot be misunderstood.

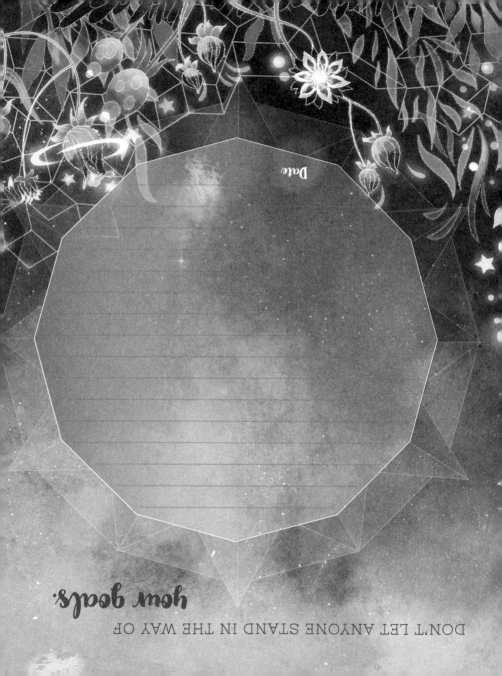

Date

DON'T LET ANYONE STAND IN THE WAY OF
your goals.

Setting a plan is great,
but never underestimate
the power of using your intuition.

Don't just look at what already is, because you might never know what could be.

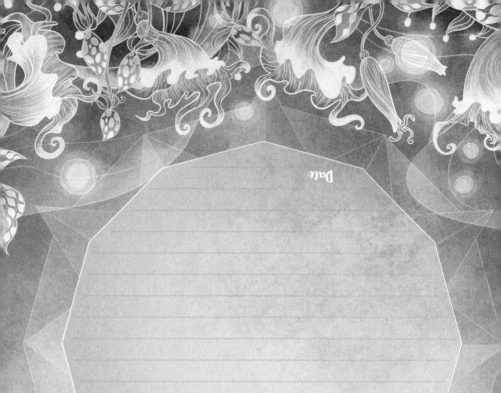

Date

The rest is up to you.

YOUR UPBRINGING IS JUST PART OF WHO YOU ARE.

Date _____

Before you can fly,
you have to realize
you've got wings.

It's good to put your needs first
once in a while. Give yourself
permission to say no sometimes!

DATE

DATE

Take aim at what you love to do,
grab it with both hands, and never let go.

Date

Be brave.

YOU DON'T ALWAYS
HAVE TO PLAY IT SAFE.
BE DARING.

Try to make the best of all
that comes your way.

ADORA

Date _____

EVERY PROBLEM HAS AN OPPORTUNITY.
YOU JUST HAVE TO BE WILLING _to find it._

When in doubt,
let your heart sing.

Date

So . . . what will you do?

PROBABLY THE ONES WHO ARE AFRAID YOU WILL.

THE ONES WHO SAY YOU CAN'T ARE

Date

Need a self-confidence boost?
Simply tell yourself,
"I can and I will."

DATE

*You will always have a friend
if you build bridges instead of fences.*

Do you think it's possible
to be too generous?

LIBBY

List five things you are grateful for today.
Now list three more.

DATE

Date _____

_____

_____

_____

_____

_____

_____

_____

_____

_____

_____

_____

_____

How'd it go?

TRY SAYING NOTHING NEGATIVE TODAY—
ABOUT YOURSELF OR ANYONE ELSE.

Date

If you're following
someone else's tracks, you're leaving
no footprints of your own.

DATE

Be responsible for creating your own happiness.
Nobody else will do it for you.

Date

waste your time.

DON'T SPEND TOO MUCH TIME WORRYING ABOUT
THINGS YOU CANNOT CHANGE—ALL THAT DOES IS

Date

Name your top five favorite animals.

ARE YOU AN ANIMAL LOVER?

DATE

If you always take the easy read, branch out once in a while and see what you're made of.

TESSA

GUILT AND WORRY
WON'T CHANGE THE PAST
OR THE FUTURE.
It's best to be present today.

_____

_____

_____

_____

_____

_____

_____

_____

_____

_____

Date _____

Limit your expectations of others and you will always be happy when they exceed them.

Achievement is great,
but so is authenticity.

Date

Persistence pays off, so keep it up!

When life gets too complicated, simplify.
Just focus on your needs for today.

PIPER

DATE

A true friend is happy for you when you are up and is there for you when you are down.

Date

One of the most
important rules of life is to
always be yourself.

SOMETIMES YOU HAVE TO FAKE IT UNTIL YOU MAKE IT.

Date

Date

take initiative

—DON'T WAIT TO BE TOLD WHAT TO DO—

DATE _____

There are two universal languages; music and smiling. Become fluent in both.

DATE

Instead of simply thinking something's possible,
tell yourself it's probable.

THE BEST ATTITUDE TO EXUDE IS

gratitude.

_____

_____

_____

_____

_____

_____

_____

_____

_____

_____

_____

_____

_____

Date _____

Date

_Remember,
every star needs darkness
to shine._

If you can't find a way, make one.

DATE

ASTRA

What is your greatest wish? Have you said it out loud or written it down? Do it!

DATE _____

Date

YOU HAVE A PLACE IN THIS WORLD.
YOU'RE JUST AS IMPORTANT AS
anyone else.

DATE

It's easier to know where you're going
when you decide where you want to be.

Date

BE KIND TO OTHERS AS WELL AS *yourself.*

If everything seems chaotic,
take time out to just breathe.

Whether you have a lot of friends or just a few,
be sure to share your true self with them always.

GEMINI

Date

A BIT OF LAUGHTER CAN CHANGE
the course of your day.

Date _____

Do you like to grow
roots or are you comfortable
on the move?

It's important to remember that
you don't have to be right all of the time.

Date

Sometimes the best thing to do is take a long nap with a comfy blanket.

DON'T LET THE DESIRE TO CHANGE
WASTE THE PERSON
you already are.

Have you ever had to fend for yourself?
What did you learn about yourself in the process?

CASSIE

Date _____

_____

wonderful.

YOU DON'T HAVE TO BE
PERFECT TO BE

While change doesn't always feel good,
progress sure does.

Sometimes it's about what you see;
other times it's about what you're looking for.

Date

Is your upbringing different from your friends'? How?

Date

make it happen.

THE ONLY WAY TO EXPERIENCE CHANGE IS TO

Tomorrow is a new day, so make it amazing!
What will you do tomorrow?

SAGE

_____ Date _____

_____

_____

_____

_____

_____

_____

_____

_____

_____

_____

_____

Keep doing your thing!

DON'T BE TOO
CONCERNED ABOUT
ANYBODY ELSE AND
THEIR JOURNEY.

Music is the sound of feelings.
What kind of music are you feeling today?

DATE

Don't limit yourself to just one passion.
Try combining two or three and see where
that takes you.

Date

get you to your destination.

YOU DON'T HAVE TO HAVE IT ALL FIGURED OUT
TO MOVE FORWARD. YOU JUST NEED
CURIOSITY AND DETERMINATION TO

Growth occurs when you have the courage to go where you have never been.

SCARLET

Date

March to the beat of your own drum.

New drum harder.

Date

Want to have
an awesome day?
Ready, set, GO!

You have to be in it to win it.

Date

You can get through any situation by using your amazing strength and then following through.

It's okay to say no without giving
an explanation.

DATE

You will enjoy the journey more
if you laugh along the way.

GEMMA

Date

WANT TO STAND OUT FROM THE CROWD?
BE COLORFUL.
Be you.

DATE

Who you were in the past doesn't matter.
It only matters who you've become.

Date

we learn the hard way.

WE LEARN IN LIFE ARE THE ONES
SOMETIMES THE MOST IMPORTANT LESSONS

Strong people are those who can show
both kindness and honesty.

DO YOU LIKE TO COOK?

What's your go-to dish?

Date

Date _____

_____

_____

_____

_____

_____

_____

_____

_____

_____

_____

_____

_____

_____

_____

_____

_____

_____

_____

you choose.

FRIENDS ARE THE FAMILY

Date

Write down your dreams, and then figure out how to make them a reality.

DATE

Sharing your knowledge with others
can often lead you to the answers more quickly.

VEGA

Date

YOU CAN'T GO WRONG IF YOU ARE DOING WHAT IS
right for you.

Your stories are important.
Write them down.

IF YOU'RE TOO AFRAID TO START,
YOU'RE ALREADY FINISHED.
DON'T LET FEAR STOP YOU FROM STARTING

something new.

Date

What kind of energy do you radiate?
Remember: positive energy reaps positive rewards.

SAGE

Date

DON'T PROMISE IT. *Prove it!*

Date

On your way to the top,
don't forget to enjoy yourself.

Met challenges head-on instead of chasing them.

Date _____

_____

_____

_____

_____

_____

_____

_____

_____

_____

_____

_____

more than you know.

YOU ARE CAPABLE OF

You can be your own hero.
Rewrite the story that way.

Date

YOURS

Don't waste today in worry, because tomorrow will come quickly and you need to be ready.

DATE

SCARLET

If you could get an MVP award for anything, what would it be?

Date

a positive life.

A POSITIVE MIND +
POSITIVE ENERGY =

HAVING IT ALL DOESN'T NECESSARILY MEAN
YOU'RE COMPLETE. CAN YOU NAME SOMETHING THAT
you're still striving for?

Date

Date

Generosity breeds gratitude,
for both the giver
and the getter.

Do you know what it's like to live in someone else's shadow?

Being "on" all the time can get exhausting.
Take time to wind down.

What talents do you have that make you stand out from the crowd?

DATE

Date

EVERY FAMILY IS *unique.*

Date

Sometimes
the quietest people have the
loudest minds.

Are you a rule follower or breaker?
Name a time when you broke the rules and
why it was important for you to do it.

Date

THE WORST THING ISN'T FAILING;
it's not trying.

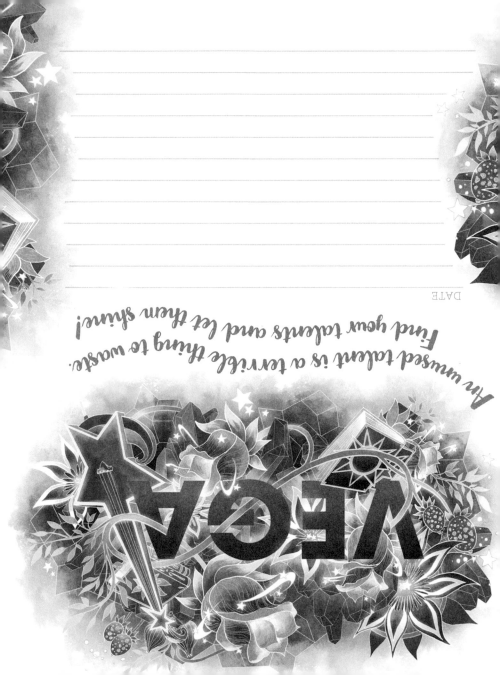

An unused talent is a terrible thing to waste.
Find your talents and let them shine!

VEGA

Date

A mind works best when it's open.
Then the sky's the limit.

THE PATH TO SUCCESS ISN'T ALWAYS SMOOTH.
IT'S DURING THOSE ROUGH PATCHES THAT
YOU REALLY LEARN WHAT YOU'RE MADE OF.

Stay strong!

_____

_____

_____

_____

_____

_____

_____

_____

_____

_____

_____

_____

Date _____

_____

_____

_____

_____

_____

_____

_____

_____

_____

_____

_____

_____

_____

_____

_____

_____

_____

_____

_____

_____

_____

_____

_____

**You can save yourself a lot of apologies
if you take a moment to think before you speak.**

Dreams can and do come true.
Have you ever had a dream that actually came true?

SAGE

Date

Be who you wish to be, not what others want to see

LOOK IN THE MIRROR—

that's your biggest competition!

_____ Date

_____

_____

_____

_____

_____

_____

_____

_____

_____

_____

_____

_____

_____

It's a very freeing moment
when you can laugh at yourself.
Try it sometime.

Date

START YOUR DAY
WITH
enthusiasm.

Date

what you feel.

IN MUSIC, PRACTICE MAY MAKE PERFECT, BUT PLAY

DATE

Beauty starts on the inside.

Date

Have you feelings
ever been hurt by someone
else's humor?

Date

ONE OF THE HEAVIEST THINGS TO CARRY AROUND IS
A GRUDGE. LETTING IT GO WILL MAKE YOU FEEL

lighter and brighter.

How is your family different from your friends' families?

DATE

MAKE YOUR SMILE CHANGE THE WORLD, BUT
NEVER LET THE WORLD CHANGE *your smile.*

Date

You will be respected for it.

HAVE THE COURAGE TO STAND UP
FOR WHAT YOU BELIEVE IN.

Let the small stuff go and
you'll have more room for the good stuff.

Date

Being a good listener is the sweet way to becoming well-spoken.

Don't underestimate yourself
and nobody else will, either.

While striving for perfection,
keep in mind that nobody's perfect.

_____
_____ Date _____
_____
_____
_____
_____
_____
_____
_____
_____
_____
_____
_____
_____

to thrive.

NEVER LOSE YOUR AMBITION

Date

make the world your own.

USE IT TO YOUR ADVANTAGE TO

DON'T LET TIME PASS YOU BY,

DATE

It's not weak to admit
you have weaknesses; it's honest.

Date

EVERY DAY IS
ANOTHER CHANCE TO
MAKE SOMETHING
WONDERFUL HAPPEN.

Date

What's one area
in life where you have a lot
to learn?

DATE

Don't let an opportunity pass you by.
Be ready when it knocks on your door.

LEONA

Whatever you create is yours.
No one can take that away from you.

Date _____

_____
_____
_____
_____
_____
_____
_____
_____
_____
_____
_____
_____
_____
_____
_____
_____
_____

Believe it.

YOU ARE STRONG AND UNSTOPPABLE. FEEL IT.

DATE

Remember that bad days do happen, but they never last.

ADORA

DATE

When life shuts a door, all you have to do
is kick open another one.

Date

When you're
all alone, how do you
entertain yourself?

To truly forgive someone is a gift. Learn to
forgive yourself and you can let go of regrets
that may be holding you down.

DATE

You get what you get,
and it's up to you to make it awesome.

If you're struggling, ask for guidance.
You'll be surprised by how willing others
are to lift you up when you need it.

Date

when one presents itself.

OPPORTUNITIES OFTEN COME FROM CHAOTIC SITUATIONS. GO WITH THE FLOW AND BE READY

Date

DON'T WORRY WHAT OTHERS ARE
THINKING ABOUT YOU. THEY'RE TOO BUSY
WORRYING WHAT YOU'RE THINKING
about them.

Don't listen to too many people—
your own voice is the most important.

DATE

You're not in competition with anyone when you're learning to be yourself.

Ask for the right words
and they will come.

CASSIE

Date

Life isn't about getting it
right all of the time. It's about the
journey along the way.

You can make your dream a reality
if you wake up and get to work.

_____ Date

_____

_____

_____

_____

_____

_____

_____

_____

_____

_____

_____

_____

_____

the courage to find them.

THEY ARE ALREADY WITHIN YOU–YOU JUST NEED

YOU DON'T ALWAYS HAVE TO REACH FOR THE STARS.

Date

Do you daydream often? What about?

DATE

*Conflict is inevitable.
What matters most is how you deal with it.*

SAGE

It's difficult to find happiness
if you don't appreciate what you already have.

Date

A great leader not only
knows the way, but shows the way. When have
you been a leader?

IN LIFE, YOU HAVE
TO TAKE THE BAD
WITH THE GOOD.
IT'S IMPORTANT TO
LEARN FROM THE BAD
AND BE GRATEFUL FOR
every bit of the good.

_____

_____

_____

_____

_____

_____

_____

_____

_____

_____

_____

Date _____

_____
_____
_____
_____
_____
_____
_____
_____
_____
_____
_____
DATE

Make sure your actions line up
with your values.

Date

Don't say it—prove it!

_____

_____

_____

_____

_____

_____

_____

_____

_____

_____

_____

_____

_____

Embrace who you are!

REMEMBER, IMPERFECTION
ISN'T A CRIME.

"If you tell yourself "I can't,"
you've already lost.

Date

Exciting things begin where your comfort zone ends!

_____
_____
_____
_____
_____
_____
_____
_____

DATE

If you have an independent spirit,
let it soar!

DATE

Give more and expect less.
Think about how much happier that will make you!

_____ Date

_____

_____

_____

_____

_____

_____

_____

_____

_____

_____

_____

Believe.

GOOD THINGS ARE GOING TO HAPPEN.

Date

Change is constant,
so why not embrace it?

When you're feeling really down,
just remember that a year from now,
whatever it is won't seem as bad.

DATE

on you.

KEEPING YOURSELF CLOSED OFF FROM OTHERS
MEANS YOU'LL MISS OUT ON LOTS OF WAYS
TO CONNECT—AND PEOPLE WILL MISS OUT

Life moves really fast, so make it a point to take time out to celebrate.

It's best to face the music
even if you don't like the tune.

CLOVER

Date

GREATNESS DOESN'T HAVE TO BE *big.*

DATE

Have you ever been called stubborn?
Why?

Date

_____

_____

_____

_____

_____

_____

_____

_____

_____

_____

_____

how far you've come.

DON'T FOCUS ON WHAT YOU
HAVEN'T DONE. MARVEL AT

The best way to gain self-confidence is by
doing what you've been afraid to do.

DATE

CASSIE

Date

create the reality you want.

REMOVE THE WORDS "I SHOULD HAVE."
FROM YOUR THOUGHTS ABOUT THE PAST. FROM
THIS MOMENT ON, STATE "I WILL . . ." AND

IT DOESN'T HAVE TO
BE ABOUT YOU ALL OF
THE TIME. SOMETIMES
MAKING ROOM FOR
OTHERS WILL ALLOW
YOU TO SHINE

even brighter.

Date

Date

Ambition can be
an amazing life force. What is your
greatest ambition?

Where do you want to be tomorrow?
Is what you're doing today going to take you there?

Date

Be yourself.

DON'T WASTE TIME TRYING TO
BE LIKE SOMEONE ELSE.

In your group of friends,
what role do you play?